No Room For Napoleon

For all my family and friends in Maine.
Remember Fred!

NO ROOM FOR NAPOLEON
A RED FOX BOOK 978 0 099 45153 2 (from January 2007)
0 099 45153 0

First published in Great Britain by The Bodley Head,
an imprint of Random House Children's Books

The Bodley Head edition published 2006
Red Fox edition published 2006

1 3 5 7 9 10 8 6 4 2

Copyright © Adria Meserve, 2006

The right of Adria Meserve to be identified as the author of this work has been
asserted in accordance with the Copyright, Designs and Patents Act 1988.

Red Fox Books are published by Random House Children's Books,
61–63 Uxbridge Road, London W5 5SA,
a division of The Random House Group Ltd,
in Australia by Random House Australia (Pty) Ltd,
20 Alfred Street, Milsons Point, Sydney, NSW 2061, Australia,
in New Zealand by Random House New Zealand Ltd,
18 Poland Road, Glenfield, Auckland 10, New Zealand,
and in South Africa by Random House (Pty) Ltd,
Isle of Houghton, Corner Boundary Road & Carse O'Gowrie,
Houghton 2198, South Africa

THE RANDOM HOUSE GROUP Limited Reg. No. 954009
www.kidsatrandomhouse.co.uk

A CIP catalogue record for this book is available from the British Library.

Printed in Singapore

No Room For Napoleon

Adria Meserve

RED FOX

Napoleon was a small brown dog with very big ideas.
One day, while he was out on his boat exploring,
he spotted land through his telescope.
"Perfect!" he said. "My very own paradise island!"

And he rowed ashore.

Napoleon strode up the beach.

Crab, Bunny and Bear came out to greet him. "Welcome," they said. Crab gave Napoleon a beautiful pebble from the beach. Bunny hung a garland of flowers round his neck, and Bear invited him on a tour of the whole island.

Later, the
friends made
Napoleon a meal
fit for a king.

"Isn't this wonderful!" said Bear.
"The best," said Napoleon. "I'd like to stay."
Crab, Bunny and Bear were delighted.
"Let's make you a home!" they said.

Napoleon got very excited.
"I want it to be tall . . .

. . . and **wide** . . .

. . . with a great ocean view!"

Napoleon had so many ideas that he **scoffed down** his dinner as quick as he could and *rushed off* in search of

. . . just the right place!

"Why is he in such a hurry?" asked Crab.
"No idea," said Bunny.
"Never mind," said Bear. "Let's play!"

Early the next morning, Napoleon was already
busy building his new home.
Crab, Bunny and Bear offered to help.

Napoleon gave his new friends orders.

"Bear, bring me some branches!"

"Bunny, fetch some flowers!"

"Crab, pile up some pebbles!"

"He sounds very important," thought the three friends. So they collected and stacked, while Napoleon chopped and hammered.

As the friends did more and more, Napoleon did less and less. But . . .

he always kept an eye on them through his

telescope.

The one time Crab, Bunny
and Bear stopped to play,
Napoleon barked:

"Jump to it! There is no time to waste!"

Napoleon made Crab, Bunny and Bear work all through the day and all through the night.

Napoleon's
house grew

bigger . . .

and bigger . . .

. . . and bigger.

Crab, Bunny and Bear's island got smaller and smaller, until
the woods, gardens and beach had nearly disappeared.

At last Napoleon's new home was finished. He stood at the top and shouted:

"I'm the King of the Castle!"

"What is he talking about?" asked Crab. "No idea," said Bunny. "All I know is that he has used up everything on the island," said Bear, "and . . .

. . . there is no room left for us."

Crab, Bunny and Bear
knew they had to
do something.

The next morning, King Napoleon
looked down from his castle.
"**Where's my breakfast?**" he said,
searching for his three friends . . .

. . . with his telescope.

No Crab . . .

No Bunny . . .

No Bear . . .

At last, Napoleon spotted them far out at sea.

King Napoleon strutted around
his kingdom. He dug holes,
he rolled in the dirt, he barked
and he howled, but no one
brought him his breakfast.

Napoleon looked for the three friends again.
They were on another island – having
A MEAL FIT FOR A KING.

"This isn't much fun!" he said.

His tummy rumbled.

Napoleon decided to row
across to the other island to
see his friends. But when he
tried to row ashore, they said:

"No! There's no room for Napoleon!"

No one had ever said 'no' to Napoleon before. "But why?" he asked.

"You used up all the pebbles and the trees and the flowers,"
said Crab.

"You wouldn't let us play,"
said Bunny.

"You spoiled our island,"
said Bear.

"You're a selfish dog!"
they all said.

Napoleon's ears drooped and his crown slid from his head. He forgot all about being king.

"It's no fun on the island without you," he said. "If I put everything back the way it was will you come home?"

"Maybe," said Crab.
   "I'm not sure," said Bunny.
      "You would have to make
         a lot of changes . . ." said Bear.

Napoleon got very excited.

"I'll knock the castle down!"

"I'll plant the most beautiful flowers!"

"I'll grow the tallest trees!"

Crab, Bunny and Bear
were delighted. They helped
to collect seeds and plants to take back.
Then Napoleon climbed into
his boat and waved goodbye.
"You'll be able to come home soon!"
he promised.

Napoleon worked and worked and worked. When the friends finally came home they couldn't believe their eyes! There were lush green trees and the most colourful flowers.

"This is even better than before!"
the three friends said.
"Isn't our island beautiful!" said Bear.

"THE BEST!" said Napoleon.
"If there's room, I'd love to stay!"

"Of course you can!" the friends said.
"Now – let's **play**!"

But far out at sea . . .
a small ginger cat
spotted land through
her binoculars.
"Purrfect," she said,
"my very own
paradise island . . ."

Other books by
Adria Meserve:

Smog the City Dog

Cleopatra Silverwing

Other books to enjoy:

G.E.M. by Garry Parsons

Billy's Bucket by Kes Gray and Garry Parsons

Biscuit Bear by Mini Grey

A Pipkin of Pepper by Helen Cooper

Eat Your Peas by Kes Gray and Nick Sharratt

Mile-High Apple Pie by Laura Langston and Lindsey Gardiner

Eric and the Red Planet by Caroline Glicksman